"I smiled with every page. This collection of whimsical fables, fun and fantastic, can be devoured in one sitting. From the sladlours, to the frupnids eating garshun seeds, to the enthused trobligors and the arguing cojolitors—a great romp. And it deftly answers that burning question: Just how many toes does a fekkerash have?"

— *Jean Rabe, author of the Piper Blackwell mysteries*

"Fables like you've never experienced before from a world you never even imagined—a place strange and alien, yet familiar. These charming stories beguile and entertain, disturb and comfort. They'll change your perspective (and your life) for the better."

— *Stephen D. Sullivan, award-winning author of*
Manos: The Hands of Fate

"Aesop, you've met your match in Dexter Dogwood, who is either a visionary author *or* an ingenious de-coder/ translator/transcriber. The lessons that this book offers to humankind—and that humankind had damned well better learn!—ring as true as any that the Ancient Greek fabulist imparted. Moreover, these tales aren't 'just' smart, savvy, entertaining, thought-provoking, relevant, and beautifully composed; they're also moving. Head *and* heart are both fully engaged. About to read *Fables from Elsewhere*? Lucky you!"

— *Paul McComas, award-winning author of*
Unforgettable, *from his Foreword*

# FABLES
## FROM
# ELSEWHERE

Written & Illustrated
by
Dexter Dogwood

Edited & with a Foreword
by
Paul McComas

Walkabout Publishing • 2016

Walkabout Publishing
S.D. Studios
P.O. Box 151
Kansasville, WI 53139
www.walkaboutpublishing.com

Cover illustration by Dexter Dogwood, inspired by illustrations within the data stream received at [*location classified*] on [*date classified*]

Cover & interior design by Stephen D. Sullivan

Special thanks to Heather McComas for help proofing.

ISBN: 978-1-5405-0446-3

Printed in the USA.

My sincerest appreciation to
Paul McComas
for his tremendous encouragement and enthusiasm.
If not for all of his help and guidance,
this work would never have seen the light of Tarsaillius.
Thank you, Paul!

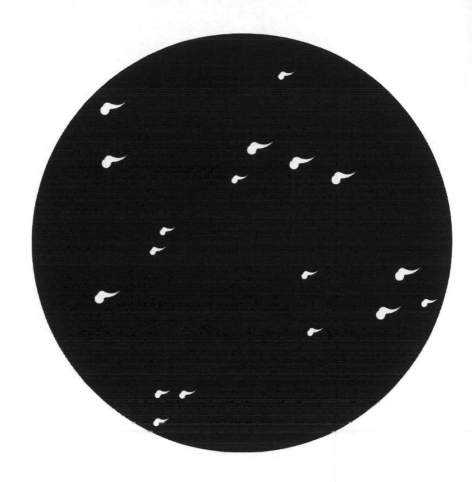

This work is humbly dedicated to all of the
intelligent, benevolent beings

*. . . out there.*

# CONTENTS

Foreword: "Life Lessons: Timeless, Universal …
and Inter-Univers-al" ................................................................11
Introduction ...............................................................................19

FABLES FROM ELSEWHERE.....................................................25

1. The Old Sladlour, the Young Sladlour, and the Swarm .......27
2. The Fekkerash, the Frupnid, and the Dagger Worm............33
3. The Rakwals and the Snerfet Farmer....................................39
4. The Trobligor and the Lantern Iglabite ...............................45
5. The Sagowump Who Saw the Sky.........................................49
6. Warm Methane Makes Better Grak ......................................55
7. The Lispadid, The Clurrabite, and The Germ ......................61
8. Making the Grand Decision...................................................67
9. The Sladlour, the Clurrabite, and the Dagger Worm ...........73
10. The Trobligor, the Frilliquat, and the Other Trobligor.....81
11. The Chubongoango Run .....................................................87
12. The Blind Kowchost and the Fekkerash .............................91

Author's Note ............................................................................97
A Sampling of (Partial) Explanations ........................................99
Disclaimer..................................................................................101
About the Author.......................................................................102

# FOREWORD

## LIFE LESSONS: TIMELESS, UNIVERSAL ... AND INTER-UNIVERS-AL

"Look past today's needs to tomorrow's—and beyond."

"Don't underestimate those you don't know or understand."

"Imitation leads to dead ends ... maybe even to death. But your *true* self—and even your deficiencies—can lead to success ... maybe even to survival."

"Honesty's not just 'the best policy'; it's also a gift to others—one that's often returned."

"Conformity blinds societies, states—even whole *species*. And silence sustains and perpetuates that blindness."

11

"Sometimes, the solution is right there in the 'solution'—the *liquid*: beer, grak, or whatever. So, ferret out the 'fly (or slime slubber) in the ointment.'"

"Others may not possess your gifts and skills, but they have different ones. Respect these ... or, ignore them—to your detriment."

"Those locked into pointless conflict and unprofitable competition miss out on opportunities—thereby *handing* opportunities to perceptive (and discreet) others."

"Teamwork and collaboration beat combat and predation."

"Look before you leap—*and* before you eat!"

"A team wins, or loses, depending on its leader."

"Love and friendship conquer, well, *almost* all. And when they don't conquer, they still yield a moral victory ... and an honorable end."

Aesop, *Shmaesop*! (Or, at least: Aesop, you've met your match!) For, the lessons I've summarized above—all of which this book's publisher, Walkabout, wisely offers herein to humankind (and all of which humankind had damned well better learn!)—ring as true as any that the Ancient Greek fabulist/storyteller himself imparted, way back when.

Another link between Aesop's and these fables: in both cases, the attributed authors may well be apocryphal. But I'm not here to determine if determined-as-hell Dexter Dogwood is a visionary scribe, or if he's "merely" an ingenious *tran*scriber, de-coder, and translator.

After all, does it even matter?

As a *very* minor Shakespeare scholar, I take issue with Bard-of-Avon deniers. My friend Michael York is one of them. Arguably, as a Shakespearean-trained actor, he ought to know; still, *I* believe ol' Will to be the authentic author of all of the works credited to him.

As with Shakespeare, so with Dogwood: I'd suggest, Lear-like, that we "reason not" who is/was real, nor who wrote (or translated) what! For, at the end of the day—or thaw, or cycle, or Season of Living—it's the tales themselves that count.

The tales—and the characters.

And the themes.

And the insights.

...And the language deftly deployed to bring *all* of the above vividly to life—and to light, even in the Season of Darkness ... a Season that, whether "real" (as depicted within *Fables from Elsewhere*) or not, is all too real in our own oft *unenlightened* world.

Wait. Did I just compare Dogwood to Shakespeare? You bet your ass (or your ass-headed "Rude Mechanical" from *A Midsummer Night's Dream* ... or your local Frupnid's freshly grown carapace), I did!

For, in the case of both the Bard's vast canon and the far shorter Double-D stories-suite (itself, by the way, but one volume, out of ten diverse ones) that you—*lucky* you!—are about to read, the tales woven impart timeless, invaluable, universal and even *inter*-Univers-al lessons. Not only are these fables, like Shakespeare's plays, utterly relevant in today's 21st-Century world— but we ignore them at our peril.

To take one example: Surely, the opening fable's cautionary message of "Look past today's needs to tomorrow's—and beyond" is a timeless yet usually ignored one (albeit *not* by North America's indigenous people: "Act with an eye toward the Seventh Generation beyond our own."). It's also a message we *must* heed, lest human-caused global warming necessitate a mass, across-space migration of humans to the Tarsaillius system. (We'd better bring presents!)

And, speaking of presents: "Others may not possess your gifts and skills, but they have *different* ones..." I believe that our human race, indeed our very planet, will either survive-then-thrive, or fail-then-fall, based largely on whether we build either walls or bridges *vis-a-vis* our current areas of division: sex/gender identity, race, ethnicity, sexual orientation, religion (or absence thereof), nationality, dis-/ability status, physical appearance, etc. If we follow the cited fable to its logical end, then we see that the recognition of diversity, and of the gifts it affords, has the power to heal the world—theirs, *and* ours.

Moreover—and, again: just as with Shakespeare—these stories aren't "just" smart, savvy, entertaining, thought-provoking, relevant, and beautifully composed (each of these attributes being a huge accomplishment in and of itself); they're also moving. Head *and* heart are both fully engaged.

You see, as much as I'm stirred by Edmund's "Nature, Thou Art My Goddess" soliloquy in *King Lear* Act I, Scene 2 (..."Why 'bastard', wherefore base? / When my dimensions are as well compact / My mind as generous, and my shape as true / As honest madam's issue?..."), I would place *Fables'* glorious finale, "The Blind Kowchost and the Fekkerash," right alongside Edmund's monologue. Yeah, "The B.K. & the F." is gonna move ya, all right...

*But...* Don'tcha *dare* skip ahead! There's a reason why, in my capacity as Dexter's editor, I insisted on which fable must go last: because this mini-masterpiece (just under 1,000 words) proves most effective, and most affecting, if preceded by all of the other tales.

Ah, but I've yet to mention the illustrations! Again: whether Dex-drawn, or legitimate alien art—"Fine word, 'legitimate'!" sneers Edmund later in his soliloquy (Sorry!)—these evocative compositions are perfect for *Fables'* purposes.

For, like the works of one of my favorites among our own planet's painters, Wassily Kandinsky, *Fables'* illos occupy that peculiar, pulsing place at the juncture of representation and abstraction. And that Land of the Liminal is, finally, the realm of the *magical.*

Just ask the shaman while he's contemplating—much as *you'll* soon contemplate these unique graphics—the waterline around a partially submerged rock: a line, at once, both water *and* rock. Or ask the voodooist at the moment when, having stepped (or leapt) onto a sacred *veve* (an intricate, mandala-like grain pattern that she herself helped create atop the naked earth), she commences dancing this divine design into oblivion.

Or, for that matter: Ask the jeskaster!

But, enough.

A brief book demands a brief Foreword (well, brief-*ish*, with—Apologies!—tons of tangents and asides ... for instance: How do you tell a legitimate [what, *that* again?], published book, like this one, from a *self*-published one? The former may have a Foreword; the latter may have a "Forward" [sic].) (Meaning: Sell That Book "Back[ward]!")

Again, and finally: *Enough!* Move along, promptly, to the good stuff. Just let me close with the Native-American saying that long has served as the core of my own conception of, and approach to, fiction writing:

"The events I'm about to share with you may or may not have happened...

"But the story is true."

— Paul McComas
Evanston, Illinois
November 2016

# INTRODUCTION

An alien civilization trying to establish contact with our own would first need simply to get our attention.

The most logical way of doing this would start with the transmission of a series of specific numbers (primes, perhaps)—a repeating sequence of pulses containing combinations not normally emitted in nature. This signal would likely be accompanied by a greeting and, perhaps, would be followed by instructions about how to respond.

In the case of the message that I've transcribed upon the following pages—a transmission that was received nearly [*number classified*] decades ago—the absence of any introductory sequence whatsoever probably means that the message was not intended for us.

How on Earth (literally), then, did we stumble upon it?

Consider two distant worlds that have already established communication and—if all has gone well thus far—commenced friendly relations. They likely would undertake the sharing of information about their respective habitats, histories, cultures, folklore, technology, and so forth.

They direct their broadcasts toward each other ... but, because radio waves expand with distance, much of a given signal not only reaches the intended recipient, it also passes *beyond* the targeted destination and continues on through space, over an immense period of time—easily, long enough for the originating planet's host star to have burned out and, in its death throes, to have taken the rest of the system with it!

Eventually, *another* world (namely ours) likewise populated by sentient creatures (namely *us!*) might detect one of these weak signals ... *and* detect within it a fragmented transmission.

On [*date classified*], a radio signal was indeed received at [*location classified*] here on Earth. It was recorded and marked as a possible extraterrestrial-to-human communication—a First Contact; a Close Encounter of the Second

Kind, arguably, by proxy. At that time, though, the signal was assumed to be impossible to decode.

Back when I was a (much) younger man, I searched for and located the original recording within the archives of [*location classified*], and I converted it, *in toto*, into digital information. Trial and, especially, error, plus numerous unsuspecting (if progressively capable) home computers, plus 14 years of work, at last resulted in a pattern that made sense: an alphabet with 209 letters, forming words that average 7.4 letters each.

However, I found that my de-code worked on only a small fraction of the transmission's full length. For all I know, my derived material is nothing more than the result of a *single* proverbial monkey with a typewriter.

There is no way of determining what the sender's/senders' words sound like (that is, if they ever have been, or even could be, vocalized)—nor, for that matter, whether the being/s who composed and transmitted the material engage/s in verbal communication with one another at all.

I have chosen familiar sounds from various human languages—leaning, I confess, toward my native English—and I've arranged them in a way intended to make the aliens' language functional for us.

The next step, of course, was translation. Fortunately, this alien language operates via a stream of ideas, much as do our sundry human "tongues." The trouble lies in *lack of reference*—the absence of, as it were, an interplanetary Rosetta Stone.

In an Earth book that mentions a horse, the word "white" or "brown" may be included (and immediately understood—on Earth, at least), but the horse is not otherwise described ("four-legged," "hoofed," "maned," etc.), since most earthlings already know what a horse looks like.

Conversely—and unfortunately—no one here on Earth could hope to describe the appearance (let alone the color!) of a *trobligor*. (Granted, the highly stylized images retrieved alongside the alien text, and included herein, prove to be of some *small* help in this regard.)

Still more trial and error—utilizing ever-newer equipment and ever-more-sophisticated linguistic algorithms—finally "excavated" and then unveiled the series of tales that follows.

It has been, and continues to be, my great honor to both undertake and continue to develop this pioneering project. I hope that, upon finishing your reading of it, you will deem my considerable expenditure of time, effort, and perspiration to have been worthwhile.

# FABLES
## FROM
# ELSEWHERE

# 1.

# THE OLD SLADLOUR, THE YOUNG SLADLOUR, AND THE SWARM

When the suns finally rise and the thaw comes, the sladlours burrow their way out of the dirt. Each finds a tlinger bush to call home for the Season of Living.

After one particularly late thaw, the first sladlour to emerge was an old one. He had large wrinkle-folds in his sides and scars on his front from many years of climbing through tlingers. He selected a small bush for his home and set to work at once, eating the nectar hairs off its razor-sharp spines.

Soon, a younger sladlour arrived to claim a much larger tlinger bush next to the old sladlour's small one. The young sladlour immediately made himself comfortable: he found a shady central spot in which to nest, with convenient low-hanging branches to nibble on. He watched the old sladlour for a while, then called out to him, "Why are you eating so much—and from such a small bush?"

The old sladlour replied, "You would be wise to get started on your own bush before the swarm gets here, my friend. The nectar hairs attract them, you know."

"The swarm could never get into this bush," the young sladlour replied. "It is too big, too deep—and I shall be here in the center. You should have chosen this bush for yourself when you had the chance."

"That bush is too big for me—and it is too big for you, too. When the swarm gets here, it will get into that bush." Even as he spoke, the old sladlour knew that his words were falling on deaf ears.

"Why should I believe you?" the young sladlour snapped back.

"Because," said his elder, "I am still alive."

The young sladlour went silent, and for a moment there was a glimmer of hope in the old sladlour's mind. It passed, though, as the young sladlour simply shrugged and rolled over.

Many cycles later, the old sladlour's bush was nearly bare; only the lowest branches still carried nectar hairs. The old sladlour was bloated almost to the point of immobility, and his front was speckled with droplets of his own blood. The young sladlour laughed at him, but the old sladlour just brushed off his taunts. For in the distance, he could hear a sickening drone: the swarm was coming. Calmly, he went about his business, knowing that he had just enough time to complete his feeding.

As the young sladlour heard the sound, it made his crest curl. He suddenly felt unsure. Doubting his previous assessment, he started eating ravenously. The sound grew louder. He looked over at the old sladlour, who had completely finished stripping his bush and now lay motionless on his back in the very center. The young sladlour panicked and began to make his way toward the old sladlour's bush, but it was too late: the swarm had already begun to surround his own bush. Drawn by the nectar, they fell upon it like rain. Wave after wave of them were impaled on its spines—yet there seemed to be no end to them. Gradually, the bush's defenses were being blunted by corpses.

After what seemed an agonizingly long period of time, the inevitable happened: the swarm frenzied, devouring everything in their path, *everything*—even their own dead. Once they had rendered the bush utterly bare, they rose up from it and moved on. Soon, they were nothing more than a distant drone, growing ever quieter.

The young sladlour was nowhere to be seen.

The old sladlour righted himself and crawled over to the safety of the larger tlinger bush.

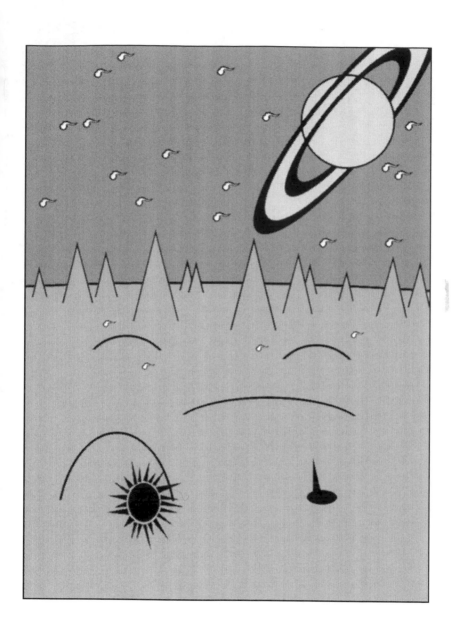

# 2.
# THE FEKKERASH, THE FRUPNID, AND THE DAGGER WORM

At the end of the Season of Living—when the kowchost have all gone, the sladlours are safe in the ground, and all that is left of the garshun plant is the single, huge seed it produces each year—that is when groups of fekkerash scour the land for anything they can use. They look for shelter, objects with which to defend their shelters, and things to eat. It is said that they will eat anything except rocks.

One group happened upon a small frupnid, gnawing on a garshun seed. The largest fekkerash immediately tried to intimidate the frupnid with posture, look—and words: "You will never be able to eat that entire seed!" he said with curled lip. "Why don't you give it to us?"

"I believe," replied the frupnid meekly, "that I can eat the entire seed myself."

"Well, perhaps I should just take it from you." And the fekkerash began to advance.

Suddenly a long, sharp point thrust up out of the ground in front of him, accompanied by a face—the face of a dagger worm. "It would seem," said the worm while extricating himself from the dirt, "that what we have here is a challenge."

"Why do you want to get mixed up in this?" the big fekkerash demanded, trying not to look weak in the face of his deadly foe.

"Entertainment!" the dagger worm cheerfully replied. "I love a good contest. Now, all we need are the stakes. What say you, frupnid?"

The frupnid gave the matter a moment's thought, then spoke up: "If I eat this entire seed, then they have to dig me a nice burrow with strong defenses—and one for you, too."

The dagger worm turned to the big fekkerash. "Agreed?"

"All right," said the fekkerash with disgust, "but if he cannot eat the entire seed, then we get to eat what remains of it—*and* eat him. And you may not stop us."

"Agreed!" cried the dagger worm.

"Very well," assented the frupnid.

All the fekkerash gathered around to watch—although, fearing the dagger worm, they didn't draw too close.

The little frupnid set about taking large bites, and soon the garshun seed began to disappear. About halfway through, however, he stopped eating.

"I knew he couldn't do it!" the big fekkerash chortled. "There is not enough room in his shell for both the whole seed and him."

On the second point, he was correct. For suddenly, there came a loud *crack*: a long, jagged line had split the frupnid's shell—and now, it began to widen. The entire carapace opened and fell apart as the little frupnid expanded like a chubongoango. After a moment, he was twice his former height, width, and length. As his new shell hardened, he quickly finished the rest of his meal ... then looked over at those who had planned to make a meal of *him*.

The fekkerash looked back: the "little" frupnid was now easily a match for the entire gang of them. They humbly began digging a burrow at the base of a low hill. They also gathered tlinger-bush spines to install around the entrance. Nearby, they dug a burrow for the dagger worm, a bit smaller and with no defenses, since none were needed.

Soon, the big fekkerash declared the work done.

"Show me the inside," the frupnid told him, then followed the fekkerash into the burrow.

The dagger worm pointed at the smallest fekkerash, saying, "And why don't you show me *my* burrow?"

The small fekkerash entered.

Before following him in, the dagger worm turned and addressed the remainder of the group with a thin smile: "The rest of you are free to go."

# 3.

# THE RAKWALS AND THE SNERFET FARMER

When the suns are high and the ground is warm, the snerfet plants begin to sing. The rakwals living within them sing too, mimicking the snerfets—and they sing well, lest a wrong note or a harsh tone cause them to be discovered by the farmer. He tends his snerfet pillars with a trumpet stick.

One day, as the farmer walked the rows, a rakwal made a mistake in its song.

The farmer heard the error and began moving toward the pillar that had the errant rakwal in it.

Then, in a moment of insane courage, another rakwal called out to the farmer with a false note.

The farmer turned and began moving toward the second rakwal.

But before the farmer could get there, from some distance away, still another rakwal called out!

This happened several more times until finally, the farmer decided that he'd had enough. He approached the pillar from which he'd last heard a rakwal call, and he waited.

The rakwal sang his snerfet-song perfectly. He didn't dare make a mistake.

The light faded, and the wind blew, but still the farmer waited. He did not know how long a rakwal could continue to mimic a snerfet plant without error. Eventually, he became cold and hungry. He was forced to give up, at least for that day.

Upon his return home, his wife asked why he was late.

"Fatherflebbing rakwals!" he cursed, then went on to explain how they would get his attention with false notes, then sing perfectly when he approached. "I tell you, they seemed to be working together."

"Eat your dinner, and get some rest," said his wife reassuringly. "You need to clear your head."

The farmer did as his wife advised, but sleep that night was hard to come by.

The following morning, he was still flummoxed. "All I can think to do," he told his wife, "is to burn the snerfet plants."

"That will take care of the rakwals," she acknowledged, somewhat alarmed, "but then, we won't eat! Perhaps you need a new approach to solving the problem."

"What do you mean?" the farmer asked, desperate for a solution.

"Well, what is the difference between a rakwal and a snerfet plant?"

"What do you mean, 'What is the difference?' A rakwal is an animal; it moves around. Snerfet plants grow in pillars; they are stationary." Even as he spoke, he couldn't help but wonder if this line of reasoning was going anywhere.

"Rakwals have ears," she said, a glimmer in her eye. "Snerfets do not."

"And...?"

"Snerfets sing; rakwals mimic. Do you see?"

"I think so. But I can't sing."

"Exactly." She turned toward the stove and began to prepare their meal.

Then, it hit him. "Brilliant!" he cried, and ran for the door. "You are wonderful!"

"What about your breakfast?" she asked as he left.

"Breakfast?" he shouted back. "We're going to have rakwal!"

Upon arriving back at his field, where the snerfets were singing sweetly, the farmer headed straight for the pillar from which he had heard the first rakwal the day before, and he raised his trumpet stick, ready to strike. Then, he began to "sing" in the only way he could: coarsely and off-key.

Soon, he heard a rakwal. It was "singing" just as poorly as the farmer. The little mimic was quite easy to locate.

As were, in turn, each of its fellows.

The farmer and his wife had meat for weeks.

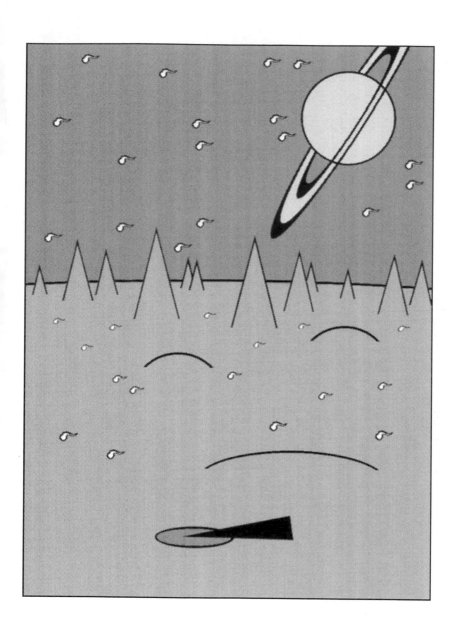

# 4.

# The Trobligor and the Lantern Iglabite

Most call it the Season of Dying; some, the Season of Darkness. Except for the distant glow of the rings of Tarsaillius, the only real light comes from the lantern iglabites. When seen from afar, a field of lantern iglabites seems to mirror the star-studded night sky above.

In addition to glowing, the lantern iglabites can smell the roots and bulbs underneath the frozen ground. Then, using their enormous body heat, they thaw the ground, dig down, and feed.

One night, a trobligor with a tlinger-bush spine sticking out of his snorkel approached one of the iglabites. "Excuse me, my good fellow. May I interest you in a very fine tlinger spine?"

"A tlinger spine?" the iglabite asked, looking slightly annoyed.

"Yes!" the trobligor enthused. "I want to trade it."

"In exchange for what?"

The trobligor forced a smile. "There is a small patch of ground I would like you to thaw for me."

The iglabite paused to think, then asked, "What could I possibly do with a tlinger bush spine?"

"You could use it for digging up roots after you have thawed the ground."

"We iglabites have been blessed with strong legs and sharp claws that are wonderful at digging. I simply don't need it."

"Then, what about for defense?" asked the trobligor eagerly. "You could use it to fight off enemies or predators!"

"I don't have any enemies, and nothing will eat me because I am poisonous." He pointed at the tlinger-bush spine. "I simply cannot think of anything I could use it for."

The trobligor's smile faded; he looked worried and spoke quickly: "All right, then, I—I'll *give* it to you."

Now, the iglabite understood. "I still don't want it," he muttered, and began to waddle away.

"And, by the way," he told the trobligor darkly, over his shoulder, "I would have been happy to pull it out of there for you—if you'd just been honest and asked me to."

# 5.
# THE SAGOWUMP WHO SAW THE SKY

**D**uring the Season of Living, most gather and prepare. The sagowumps are no exception, but unlike most creatures, they seem to be in no hurry. This is due to their fanatical belief that the sky will provide everything they need, whenever it is needed—not surprising, for all they need is moisture and organic material. *Any* organic material.

With their broad hoods, they are unfazed by the elements. These same hoods, however, make it rather difficult for sagowumps to look up at their cherished sky ... but then, they refuse to do so anyway, for fear of defiling, with a gaze, their treasured heavens. As a result, the sagowumps keep their eyes low. They recognize each other not by their faces, but by their feet.

One day, a sagowump who was returning to his village tripped and fell to the ground. Before he knew it, he had rolled onto his back. He was unable to close his eyes in time, and he glimpsed the sky. He immediately righted himself, hoping that everything would be all right.

But then, quite suddenly, he realized what he had just seen:

The sky was *green!*

He had always been told that the sky was orange; indeed, it was so written. He had even been taught that its green reflection in puddles was an optical illusion, caused by the color of methane. But now, he was filled with doubt.

The sagowump looked around to make sure that no one else was nearby, then climbed partway up a rock and raised his hood as high as he could. He peered up, and—there it was:

The sky really *was* green!

But no; no, he simply could not accept this. *The sky is orange*, he told himself. *The Writings prove it.* Then he quickly climbed back down and went about his business, instructing himself to forget about the whole thing.

Life returned to normal.

As time passed, the sagowump thought less and less about it.

Then, one day, a younger sagowump came scurrying into the village. "The sky is green! The sky is green!" he shouted.

Everyone turned away and covered their ears at the blasphemy.

The older sagowump considered coming to the young one's aid, but he held his tongues. It was well that he did, too, for he next heard the footsteps of an approaching cloptrow.

The young sagowump continued: "The sky is green! I have seen it myself! The sky is..."

*Whack! Whack! Whack!* came the distinctive sound of a trumpet stick. (Every cloptrow carries one.)

"But I..."

*Whack!*

"I really..."

*WHACK!*

The young sagowump said no more, for he now lay unconscious on the ground.

"Take him to the firmamentoreum," the cloptrow barked.

His minions rushed to carry out his orders.

"Evil has obviously taken over his mind!" the cloptrow shouted. "He cannot be trusted! We will try to help him!" Then he turned and marched off.

The older sagowump was devastated—not only by his failure to help, which shamed him, but also by this apparent confirmation that his eyes had *not* deceived him and that The Writings were, in fact, wrong.

He decided to confide in his wife, hoping that she would not leave him over his disgrace. He explained that it had been an accident; it was not his fault. "Believe me," he begged. "Don't leave me!" he pleaded.

His wife then took his hand and whispered, "I know the sky is green; I saw it when I was a young girl. When I told my mother, she made me swear to secrecy. She told me the swarm would seek me out and eat me alive if I so much as *thought* about it."

Her words made the sagowump feel better— and worse.

He decided to approach his best friend about the subject. Nervously, the friend dropped his voice and spoke of a similar experience.

He asked his parents, then his grandparents. All hesitated, but all then whispered that they knew the sky was green.

He talked to others. They all knew.

*Everyone*, it seemed, knew.

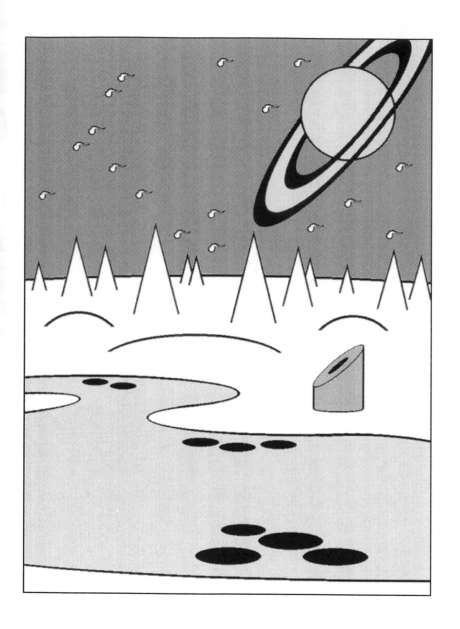

# 6.

# WARM METHANE MAKES BETTER GRAK

There once was a jeskaster who decided to make his own grak. His friend offered to help him with its production—*and* its consumption. Together, they set out to find everything that they would need.

First, they obtained a tablet that explained the grak-making process in great detail, including step-by-step instructions and checklists. The two studied it intently, to the point of memorization. They also researched other sources, looking for tricks and hints.

Next, they needed the hardware: tubes, paddles, filters, a heat source, and a Dewar flask.

All were easily obtained from the supply warehouse.

As they made their way home, they met an old snerfet farmer who recognized the equipment they had purchased. As he passed, he winked and said, "Use warm methane."

The jeskaster mentioned to his friend that he had read of this tip, adding, "It's probably true."

His friend replied, "Let's try both cold methane from the river *and* warm methane from the well. Then, we'll know for sure."

The jeskaster agreed.

When they arrived back home, they began to set up their equipment. It took several cycles to assemble everything. Once it was complete, they took a moment to marvel at their creation.

Now, they needed the raw materials. For this, they split up. One gathered dleander roots, ardygrem, and cold methane, while the other headed for the well.

Soon, they began the process of production, knowing that it would take a while before they would see any output.

After a few cycles, during which they attended to their normal duties (which helped pass the time), they met to test the results of their labor. They each sampled both batches and immediately agreed that the grak made with warm methane was the better batch.

Now, the jeskaster had an idea: "If warm methane is good, then hot methane should be even better."

His friend agreed. "We'll need to find a way to heat the methane—but if we make it *too* hot, it will evaporate."

"What if we keep it under pressure?"

"We'll need to redesign the entire apparatus to do that."

"Well then," said the jeskaster gleefully, "we'd better get started!"

After much time and expenditure, the new machine was ready. They decided to conduct a test run at full pressure—while they stood a safe distance away. Fortunately, their concern was unfounded, and they began to safely produce a complete batch. The new complications made the process a little slower, but the jeskaster insisted that it would be worth the wait. He tasted the new brew and immediately said, "This hot-methane grak is definitely better."

His friend tasted it, too. "I'm not sure," he replied, then tasted it again. "No, I don't think I can tell the difference."

"Well, I can," the jeskaster insisted. "Perhaps the snerfet farmer will give us his assessment."

"An excellent idea. Let's go and ask him."

After finding the old man and obtaining his agreement, they presented him their wares. Much to the dismay of the jeskaster, the farmer, too, could not tell the difference. Visibly frustrated, the jeskaster threw up his hands and asked, "Why is grak made with warm methane better in the first place?"

The farmer narrowed his eyes; the answer, to him, was obvious. "Because," he said flatly, "slime-slubbers don't live in wells."

# 7.

# THE LISPADID, THE CLURRABITE, AND THE GERM

As shadows grow short and the river runs clear, growth can be found everywhere. Tlinger shoots rise, the kowchost return, and female chubongoangos begin swallowing as many males as they can find. The lispadids lay traps for unsuspecting prey; once they have fed, the clurrabites eat everything the lispadids have left behind.

Lispadids and clurrabites both love the taste of early-stage garshun seeds. The germ in an unopened garshun seed is delicious, nutritious— and almost impossible to get at.

One day, a lucky lispadid found a garshun seed. He tried and tried to break through its shell, but he simply could not get into it.

A clurrabite watched him from a distance, hoping for some leftovers. When it became clear that there would be none, he began to move off.

The lispadid saw this and hailed him: "Wait a moment, my friend. Perhaps you could help me with this?"

The clurrabite turned and said, "I'm sure that you know we clurrabites make it a point to exert as little effort as possible to find food. Why should I help you, and get nothing out of it? I'd guess there's only enough inside that seed for one."

"How about a game?" the lispadid replied. "The winner gets the seed; the loser has to help open it."

"No. That sounds like too much work."

"But it's a garshun-seed germ! When was the last time you ate one? And, look: it has already begun to split."

The clurrabite paused, then asked: "What game?"

"Chekertaguckuck!" said the lispadid with enthusiasm. "You know how to play, right?"

"Of course I know how to play, but don't you think you have an advantage? You have eyes all around your body. I would never be able to sneak up on you."

"I will give you some extra time. And you can go first."

"Very well," said the clurrabite, "but what about the seed? We should put it in a safe location while we play."

"That is a very good idea," affirmed the lispadid, clutching the huge prize. "Where do you suggest we put it?"

The clurrabite gestured off to the side. "Right on the ground, in the middle of those tlinger bushes."

"Excellent! But I will need your help; I don't want to be poked by razor-sharp spines."

"Certainly. May I also suggest that we position it cracked-part-down? It will be more stable that way—less likely to roll away."

"Agreed."

The two lifted the huge seed and placed it amid the bushes cautiously, without being poked; then they moved into their starting positions for the game. "You may begin," said the lispadid. "I shall wait here for a reasonable period of time."

"All right, then; I'm off," said the clurrabite, and began moving toward a large rock. He soon disappeared behind it.

The lispadid waited for a generous period of time, then began to move toward the rock in a large arc, making his approach with great patience and skill. Once he had arrived at the rock, he peeked around it: the clurrabite was nowhere to be found. He could not understand. *Where could he have gone?* he wondered. Then he looked down: there was a depression in the ground, and the soil around it was loose. The clurrabite had burrowed into the ground!

Suddenly realizing the implications, the lispadid ran back toward the place where the seed had been hidden. He crashed through the tlinger bushes—at great expense in blood—and found, to his relief, that the seed was still there. But there was a depression in the ground underneath it, and the soil around it was loose. When the lispadid took hold of the seed and set about rolling it over, it did so far too easily, for it was much lighter now than before.

In horror, the lispadid saw that the crack in the shell was now wider than it had been—and the germ was missing.

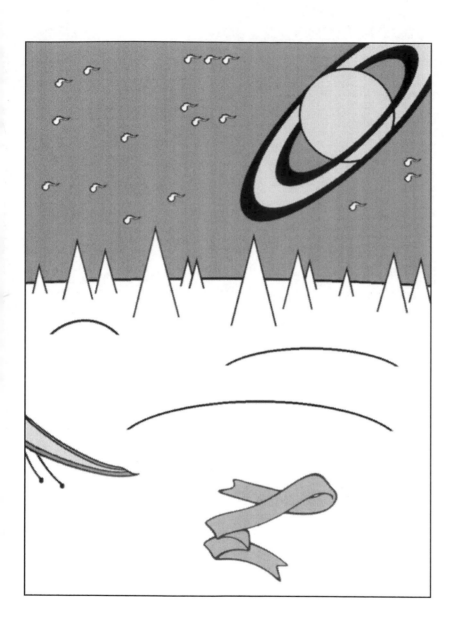

# 8.

# MAKING THE
# GRAND DECISION

When the morning moisture is no longer frozen, the time of the Grand Decision looms. There is a lot of discussion among the community about which cojolitor is right. Some cojolitors say that the snerfets should be harvested early, and they offer to help right away; others, to help later, for the flood will be delayed and the harvest can wait. Still other cojolitors argue for different strategies, though their followers are few. The choice of which cojolitor's ribbon one should accept will affect almost everything, from the snerfet crop to the chubongoango run.

As the groups of adherents become fewer and larger, individual cojolitors descend upon those who are still undecided. On one occasion, three beribboned cojolitors—a nailoht, a cloptrow, and a sagowump—descended all at once upon a lone jeskaster.

The nailoht addressed the jeskaster first: "If we don't harvest early, we risk losing crops in the flood."

The cloptrow turned on the nailoht: "I don't think you know what you're talking about."

The nailoht snapped back, "I *know* we can control the flood—but only partly. The rest is up to the rain and melt."

"And how do you know so much?"

"I have measured the depths."

"How do we know you did? You could be making that up..."

As the two argued on, the jeskaster began to lose interest and turned his attention to the sagowump, who was standing silently behind the other two with all of his arms folded across his front. His face was completely hidden, but one digit beckoned. As the jeskaster began to move around the arguing pair, they noticed and called out to him:

"You can't trust the sagowump," said the nailoht.

"Look," the cloptrow added, "you can't even see his face!"

The two then returned to their original argument:

"The likelihood of an early flood must be given consideration."

"What kind of special training do you have on the subject?"

Over and over, the nailoht spun his web of logic, and the cloptrow tore into it. But still, the sagowump said nothing.

Again, the jeskaster lost interest and turned away.

This time, the sagowump, with a shrug, offered him his ribbon.

The jeskaster stepped forward, took the ribbon, and put it on.

When they saw this, the nailoht and the cloptrow abruptly ceased arguing. "Why *him?*" they asked in unison.

"Because," replied the jeskaster, "it was the quickest way to make you two shut up. I have work to do, and your fighting doesn't help get snerfets harvested." Then the jeskaster went about his business.

Cursing under their breath, the nailoht and the cloptrow turned away. Then, fingering their ribbons, they moved on in search of the next of the undecided—with the sagowump following quietly behind.

# 9.

# THE SLADLOUR, THE CLURRABITE, AND THE DAGGER WORM

Once the warm winds have blown for many cycles, and the swarm is long gone, and life is well under way in the Season of Birth, the ground finally thaws enough for the long-distance burrowers to begin moving.

A sladlour watched in amazement as the ground erupted near his tlinger bush:

A clurrabite wriggled free of the soil and emerged. "Phew!" said he, "I almost hit your bush. That would have hurt badly."

"How do you know where you're going?" asked the sladlour.

"I have to guess," replied the clurrabite. "Although it's true that we clurrabites can sense food from below, food is *all* we can sense—and tlinger spines are not food. Speaking of food, though: you haven't seen any around here, have you?"

The sladlour thought for a moment, then gestured off to one side. "Three cycles ago, I was in that bush on the hill."

The clurrabite turned his head to follow the gesture—and smiled, for a "hill" to a sladlour is but a slight mound to a clurrabite.

"I could see," continued the sladlour, "something up there that looked like a carcass."

"Well, then," said the clurrabite, "I will just have to take a look." He began to shorten his length and widen his diameter, grunting all the while: shorter and shorter, wider and wider, until he could tip himself up and balance on one end. "Yes," he said, peering into the distance, "I believe you are correct. That does look like a carcass—perhaps of a lispadid. I certainly wouldn't mind eating one of *them*—evil flajusnits!" He tipped himself back down, hitting the ground with an undignified *plop*. "Well, it's been very pleasant and productive talking with you, my friend, but I have a lunch date with a carcass."

Just as the clurrabite began to move off, he cried out in pain and rolled over, almost hitting a tlinger bush. Blood began to stream from his underside as the spike that had impaled him continued to squirm its way out of the ground.

It was a dagger worm.

The sladlour, obviously upset, asked, "Why did you do that?"

The dagger worm looked around to see what he had done. "It was not my intention to hurt anyone. I can't see where I'm going underground, and from last season, I remembered this area to be open." He paused for a moment to think, then moved toward the front of the clurrabite and asked, "What can I do?"

"Stop the bleeding!" cried the clurrabite in a pained voice.

"I have no limbs with which to do that," said the worm, who then turned toward the sladlour. "But *he* does."

"Oh, no!" said the sladlour. "I'm not coming over there. You'll eat me!"

"First of all, I won't eat you; a leathery bag full of mush is not what I would call 'food.' What's more, I will protect you." The dagger worm added sternly, "Now, hurry!"

The sladlour reluctantly left the security of his bush and attached himself to the clurrabite's wound, doing his best to act as a patch. "Now what?" he asked.

The clurrabite's voice was strained: "Lispadid yarn ... Use lispadid yarn."

"Where do we get it?" the dagger worm asked.

The sladlour told him about the carcass, then said, "But if something comes along and eats me while you're away, this clurrabite and I will both die."

The dagger worm had a plan for that, too: "I will dig a hole just big enough for you; the clurrabite can roll upright, with you hidden underneath."

The idea did not please the sladlour, but he agreed, knowing that if necessary, he could burrow his way out.

The dagger worm quickly dug the hole, then made sure everything went well as the clurrabite righted himself. With the sladlour safe underneath, the dagger worm hurried off to retrieve the lispadid yarn.

The sladlour strained with all his strength to keep the wound closed, but blood continued to leak out. After a while, he noticed that the hole in which he was hiding was starting to fill. Time crept by as he wondered when he would be forced to abandon his post. As uncomfortable as he was, he resolved to stay until the last moment. As that moment drew near, he readied himself to make his escape.

Suddenly, the clurrabite rolled onto his side.

The sladlour peered up:

The dagger worm had returned. He had a large wad of lispadid yarn wrapped around his spike, and a bit more trailing behind him.

The sladlour, soaked in blood, could no longer hold on, but he somehow found the strength to apply the yarn to the clurrabite's wound. As the yarn came into contact with the blood, it became very sticky—so much so that the sladlour needed the dagger worm's help to free himself after he had finished.

The clurrabite rolled himself upright. "That's much better," he said, "though it's still quite painful." He rolled slightly to one side and began to move. "Come, sladlour: climb onto my back. I will do the work and take us both to the top of your 'hill.' A feast still awaits there."

The sladlour replied, "But I don't eat carcass."

"Don't worry," the clurrabite confidently said, "a feast awaits you as well."

The sladlour did as the clurrabite asked, and as he rode, he cleaned himself off. The dagger worm slithered ahead of them to claim and guard the prize.

Once all three had arrived, the clurrabite rolled the large lispadid carcass over two nearby tlinger bushes, crushing them as flat as a slime slubber. Then he pulled the two wrecked bushes out of the depression where they lay, revealing a sizable puddle of nectar hairs.

"Feed on your beloved nectar," the clurrabite instructed the sladlour. "The dagger-worm and I will be here for several cycles, feeding on this carcass, and we will see that nothing bothers you."

And they all began to eat.

# 10.
# THE TROBLIGOR, THE FRILLIQUAT, AND THE OTHER TROBLIGOR

When the ardygrem blossoms release their spores and the frupnids change color, the swarm returns—this time not to eat, but to be eaten. (By this time, however, they have been reduced to a small fraction of their earlier number.)

Two young trobligors were squabbling over an individual member of the swarm, each of them trying to claim the delicate prize as his own.

A frilliquat looked on with interest, for she found their behavior quite comical. After the trobligors had fallen over each other several times, the frilliquat decided to intervene. "Excuse me," she said. "Perhaps I could help you solve your dispute."

They both froze, and then one of them spoke up: "How would you decide which one of us gets it?"

The frilliquat replied, "I will give you some tasks, to determine who is more worthy."

"What kind of tasks?" the other asked.

"I will ask you some questions, and we will see who is right."

The trobligors agreed and waited for the first question.

"How many toes does a fekkerash have?" the frilliquat posed.

They answered in unison: "Forty-seven."

"Correct! Let's try another one: When does a rakwal sing?"

"When the snerfets do," they answered simultaneously.

The frilliquat scratched her head. "This does not seem to be getting us anywhere. Perhaps you two should go back to wrestling." She turned and started to walk away.

"Wait!" one of the trobligors shouted. "Please help us."

The frilliquat stopped and turned around. "What can I do?"

The other trobligor asked: "Is it true that you only eat dleander roots?

"Absolutely," the frilliquat replied.

The trobligors approached and together held out the battered but intact meal. "Will you hold this for us as we fight?" one asked.

"Certainly," she responded, "provided you follow my instructions."

The trobligors agreed.

The frilliquat pointed off to her left. "I want you"—she nodded toward one of the trobligors—"to start over there." Then she pointed to her right. "And I want *you*"—indicating the other trobligor—"to start over *there*. And don't begin fighting until I tell you to."

The two moved to their positions.

"Now," said the frilliquat, "look at me." As the trobligors watched, the frilliquat ripped open the carcass, spilling its contents on the ground in front of her.

The trobligors gasped in horror as they ran back to their ruined lunch, crying "Why, why?" and "What have you done?"

"What have I done? I have done you a tremendous favor!" The frilliquat calmly pointed at the innards. "Look closely: nothing but eggs. This is how the swarm reproduces: fools like you eat the carcass, and then, when the eggs hatch— the hatchlings eat *you*."

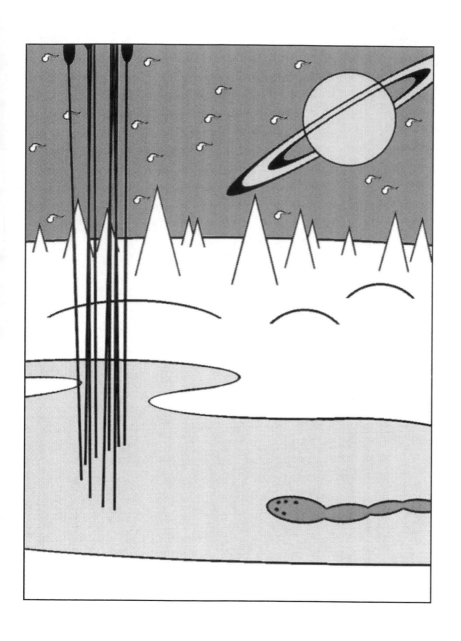

# II.
# THE CHUBONGOANGO RUN

The second cycle after the flood signals a change for all life forms upstream. The vactnowariat pods begin to hatch, the slime slubbers flee, the chubongoangos give chase—and they, in turn, are targeted for capture through the ritual contest known as the Einnidathlon, or chubongoango run.

Prior to the run, the cojolitors assign every participating group a leader. Meanwhile, the pokers practice with their pokestilts, the catchers meet at the river to coordinate their catching arcs, and the carriers lift heavy objects to ready their muscles for their burdensome quarry—because the chubongoango, when poked, puffs itself up into a very weighty creature indeed.

One time, a cloptrow was assigned to lead a certain group. Although he had no experience, his authority was absolute. The cloptrow climbed onto his stilts and, barely able to keep himself upright, led his team into the river. As the catchers formed their arc, he told them to spread out farther.

One of the catchers spoke up: "We're stationed too far apart; they'll slip through."

The cloptrow replied, "Not the biggest ones." He turned to the pokers and said, "Only poke the longest of them."

A poker answered, "We can't see the whole thing when we strike. If we wait to see where its tail ends, we won't have time to hit it."

"Try anyway," the cloptrow snapped back.

The pokers looked at each other and shrugged.

One poker tried—without success—to follow the unusual order; the rest simply ignored it. Puffed-up chubongoangos began slipping between the catchers, leaving the carriers nothing to move and stack.

Other, more successful groups had already begun to build their tumuli.

As the cloptrow moved around, repeating his pointless orders, a lucky poke found an especially large chubongoango. When it lodged between two stilts, two carriers hustled forward to pick it up.

The cloptrow immediately stopped them, saying, "One of you should be enough. Here's how to do it..."

The delivery of still more pointless orders proved too much of a delay, for the giant chubongoango relaxed and slipped through to freedom.

Finally, the catchers moved closer together. No order had been given; they did this of their own volition.

This infuriated the cloptrow; he immediately left the river, thereby disqualifying his entire team. As he climbed up the bank, he complained that they had not followed his orders. "If they had," he griped, "I'd have won!"

An older cloptrow who was watching heard this and turned toward him. "Only the team can win," he pronounced. "And only the leader can lose."

# 12.

# THE BLIND KOWCHOST AND THE FEKKERASH

Late in the Season of Living, most are hurriedly gathering. Some dig, some die, and some depart. The kowchost, after growing two sets of wings, depart—that is, unless they are unable to make the journey.

One such individual, an older garouff kowchost, was plodding his way across the furrows and digging up bulbs to eat.

"Hey, watch where you're going!" a small fekkerash said as he scampered clear.

"I'm sorry," replied the kowchost, "I didn't see you there."

"How could you not see me? I'm right in front of you."

The kowchost sighed. "I am blind. My eyesight began fading this past season, and now it is gone."

"If you can't see," inquired the fekkerash with some concern, "then how can you fly?"

"I can't fly."

"So, you are not going to migrate with the other kowchost? What are you going to do?"

The old kowchost's matter-of-fact reply: "I am going to die." And he scratched up another bulb.

"Then why are you still eating?"

"You sure do ask a lot of questions!" The blind kowchost shrugged. "Why do I eat? Because I am hungry. And what of you? Why are you all by yourself?" Then he added, just before starting to munch on his bulb, "I've never heard of a lone fekkerash."

The fekkerash sighed. "I was returning to my burrow with a tlinger spine. When I got there, a trobligor was just leaving; it had eaten the rest of my gang. I guess this means that *I'm* going to die, too. I could never hope to dig a burrow deep enough, fill it with food, and defend it through the Season of Dying, all on my own."

"Why don't you join another group of fekkerash?"

"Even if my kind were friendly, nobody wants another mouth to feed—especially not this late in the season."

"Perhaps I could help you," the kowchost suggested. "I have little else to do."

"I truly appreciate your offer, but I don't think that would work. Although you may be able to find me food, you would not be able to help me dig a safe burrow; you are much too big. And anyway, I could never defend a burrow by myself."

The kowchost smiled with both of his mouths. "Who needs a burrow, anyway? If you stay with me, you will eat, and not be eaten—and you can help me navigate."

"All right," the little fekkerash agreed with lightened heart, and leapt up on top of him.

And so, they set out together, determined to be healthy and happy for as long as possible.

At first, all went well: the little fekkerash had sharp eyes, and the kowchost had a long gait. The days were still warm and the food still plentiful. But as the light faded and the nights grew cold, the looming questions of "when" and "how" came to the fore. Neither creature relished the thought of becoming food for clurrabites.

Then, the little fekkerash had an idea: "Could you fly with me on your back?"

"Not on my back; you'd block my wing movement. Perhaps you could hang onto my front."

"Yes, and from there I could tell you which way to go."

"Perhaps—though I doubt you'd be able to do so fast enough. If I don't react very quickly, we will crash. And if I should land on top of you, my little friend...!" The kowchost shook his head.

"Well, as you said before, we have little else to do ... and little time left."

The two spent three cycles rehearsing—initially on the ground. The fekkerash learned where and how to hang onto the kowchost, as well as how to avoid shifting his weight too much or too suddenly. Then they practiced verbal signals, as the kowchost leaned this way and that. After that, they made a series of short glides into the wind.

Finally, they were ready to go. Just before the suns reached their highest point, the fekkerash latched on. The kowchost began to run and flap. A moment later, they were climbing. Higher and higher they flew. The fekkerash managed to keep the kowchost level and on course, but he found it impossible to judge distances on such a large scale, for he had only ever needed to gauge short distances while on the ground. He could not tell how high up they were, nor locate a suitable place to land.

They continued on for quite a while, but then they both began to tire. The kowchost started to glide down. The lower they got, the better the fekkerash could see—much to his horror: the ground below was jagged and unforgiving. It was all sharp peaks and deep gorges, and there was nowhere at all to land.

The fekkerash described what he saw, then fretted, "I can't hold on much longer."

"I can't hold us up much longer, either," replied the kowchost. "I was hoping that we would make it through this part of the journey to better land, but I am simply not strong enough. I'm sorry."

"Don't be," said the little fekkerash, "for I am not. We should never have made it *this* far." His hold was beginning to slip.

Sensing this, the kowchost reached down to hold the fekkerash with his feet. "You are right, my friend. We have done well: we have lived long into the Season of Dying."

"Indeed," said the fekkerash, "we have lived far longer—and far better—together than either of us could have lived alone."

"Shall I make it quick?"

"Yes, my friend. Quick."

# AUTHOR'S NOTE

This series of fables is the first completed book within a wide-ranging collection. The other represented genres are: a love story, a travelogue, science fiction (from, of course, an alien point of view), poetry, a cookbook (shall we cue Damon Knight—?), an excerpt of a mission report from an alien ship of exploration, a campfire tale, an epic saga, and an alien's musings about how other species treat their planets. What they have in common is that all derive from the same (unknown and alien) source.

The observant reader might note several details of particular interest. I shall offer no definitive answers, no "recipes" (well, except within that cookbook) ... but I perhaps will serve up a few *hors-d'oeuvres*.

You see, there are reasons why—within the fables' illustrations—the stars have tails, and the ringed planet is tilted just-so.

And what's the deal with that "nailoht" and its silent *h*? There's a reason there, too.

I will provide you with *a few* explanations...

...on the next page!

If you'd rather continue to ponder, then read no further—or, rather: go *back*, and read the fables again. For within them are plenty of clues about the tails, the tilt, and numerous other tidbits...

...Right there, for the finding...

# A SAMPLING OF (PARTIAL) EXPLANATIONS

## Spoiler Alert!

The tailed stars are not merely the result of artistic stylization. If an atmosphere is dense enough, then that atmosphere can refract light, much as a liquid does. Imagine being submerged in a swimming pool and looking up through the water: everything you see above-and-beyond the pool's surface moves in concert with the rippling movements *upon* that surface. This is the phenomenon being represented by those "star tails," within the air itself—and on a planetary scale.

**The tilt:** The originating world is actually a moon orbiting the ringed planet Tarsaillius, whose ring position shifts consistently (and in, moreover, a pattern I've worked out), according to the season. (NOTE: The fables are *not* presented in calendrical order.)

**The Nailoht:** That's "Tholian" spelled backward. In case you're unfamiliar with a certain classic 1960s sci-fi TV show, there's a popular episode titled "The Tholian Web." Please recall that, in the fable "Making the Grand Decision," the nailoht spins a kind of ... well, *you* know.

And this trio of tidbits merely scratches the (lunar) surface!

# End of Spoilers

# DISCLAIMER

Either the text preceding these few post-fables pages—Paul McComas' Foreword, plus my Intro and all of the fables—comprises an extended exercise in imagination ... or else, it's all true, and the Author's Note and Sampling constitute a kind of Roswellian cover-up. Maybe "nailoht" was my sole playful tweak of an otherwise verbally authentic transmission/ translation.

It's up to you to decide.

# ABOUT THE AUTHOR

Dexter Dogwood is a composer, vocalist, musician, photographer, graphic artist, and illustrator, as well as the author of the SF novella *The Remnant*, which was Honorably Mentioned in *Leading Edge* magazine's short-story competition. (He is seeking publication for that piece.) Other interests include woodworking, mechanical engineering, and cooking. (He *may* also be an accomplished de-coder, translator, and transcriber.)

Dexter lives in northern Illinois with his wife Pauline and their yellow Labrador retriever, "Scratchingbear."

It was not until he reached the age of 50 that Dexter—long challenged by severe dyslexia—found that dictation software had become good enough for him to finally write the longer works that had been percolating inside him for decades. "There is," says the author, "*much* of that work to now be written."

Repairing old, and creating new—that's Dexter's way of life.

# WALKABOUT PUBLISHING
## Great Stories by Great Authors

Robert E. Vardeman—Michael A. Stackpole—Marc Tassin—James M. Ward
Lorelei Shannon—Donald J. Bingle—Kathleen Watness—Paul Genesse
Tim Wagonner—Kelly Swails—Jason Mical—Kerrie Hughes—John Helfers
Brandie Tarvin—Dean Leggett—Sabrina Klein—Eric Greene—Anton Strout
E. Readicker-Henderson—Wes Nicholson—Linda P. Baker—Steven Saus
J. Robert King—Chris Pierson—Daniel Meyers—Elizabeth A. Vaughan
Jennifer Brozek—Richard Lee Byers—Brad Beaulieu—Dylan Birtolo
Paul McComas—William F. Nolan—Annette Leggett—Dexter Dogwood
Stephen D. Sullivan—Jean Rabe—*And More!*

Manos: The Hands of Fate • Unforgettable • Canoe Cops vs. the Mummy
Fit for a Frankenstein • The Crimson Collection • Manos: Talons of Fate
White Zombie • Uncanny Encounters — LIVE! • The Twilight Empire
Stories from Desert Bob's Reptile Ranch • This and That and Tales About Cats
Luck o' the Irish • Martian Knights & Other Tales • Carnage & Consequences
Fables from Elsewhere • Zombies, Werewolves, & Unicorns • Daikaiju Attack
Under the Protection of the Cow Demon • Uncanny Encounters: Roswell
Tournament of Death 1—4 • Pirates of the Blue Kingdoms • *And More!*

### Walkabout Publishing
P.O. Box 151 • Kansasville, WI 53139
www.walkaboutpublishing.com